Brooklyn Bat Boy

A Story of the 1947 Season that Changed Baseball Forever

GEOFF GRIFFIN

FOR BRADEN

First published in the United States of America - April, 2016.

GeoffGriffin.com

BrooklynBatBoy.com

Twitter - @BrooklynBatBoy

Cover Design by Kit Foster - KitFosterDesign.com

ISBN -13: 978-1530482672
ISBN - 10: 1530482674

For Kathleen, Alex, Dylan, Madeline and Evan

TABLE OF CONTENTS

CHAPTER 1

"Hey, you knuckleheads! Stop goofin' off! You comin' in, or what?"

Bobby was just inside the right field fence at Ebbets Field, looking out at Finn and James on Bedford Avenue.

"Get a load of this," Bobby said. "A fella gettin' the chance to sneak into the stadium where the Dodgers play when nobody's around don't come along every day. We don't wanna go wastin' it."

Finn and James looked scared. They were Dodger fans, but nothing like Bobby. He was the biggest Dodger fan in the whole Flatbush area of Brooklyn. He was the one who talked Finn and James into leaving their Irish-filled neighborhood to walk through Flatbush and down to Ebbets Field today. He was the one who found a space just big enough to squeeze through between two boards in the right field fence.

"We might get caught," Finn said, "and then we's done for. They'll put our names on a list tellin' the ushers not to let us into no more games. I'm only 12. I don't wanna go the rest of my life without no Dodger games."

James nodded and said, "Don't go breakin' the Devil's dishes. This could turn into a weasel deal if we get caught."

Bobby knew he had to keep talking. He pointed to the outfield grass and said, "Holy cow! That's the greenest grass you ever seen! That grass is just beggin' you to come run on it! Besides, the new Dodgers season starts next week. Once it gets goin' this place is always gonna be full of people. Come on! What's-a-matta?

"It's the first sunny day in forever and everythin's back the way it's supposed to be. We's gonna play stickball every day, and the team we call 'Da Bums' is gonna win the World Series in 1947. Before all that happens, we got our one-and-only chance to run around on Ebbets Field like we's really on the Dodgers."

Finn and James still looked scared. Bobby had one last idea. He reached into his pocket and pulled out a ring. He stuck his arm through the crack in the fence to show it to Finn and James.

"Just to make sure we got good luck, I'm gonna let you guys touch this lucky Claddagh ring. It was my grandpa's from over in County Waterford. He gave it to my Ma when she left Ireland to come live in America so she'd always have a bit of Irish luck with her. It's too big for me to wear, so I keep it in my pocket. See the heart that's below the crown and being held between the two hands? All you do is rub the heart and it gives you a bit of luck."

Bobby shook the ring in front of Finn's face.

"C'mon. Try it."

"Fine, if it'll shut your yap," Finn said and rubbed the heart on the ring followed by James.

The two boys took turns working their way through the space between the boards in the right field fence that divided Ebbets Field from Bedford Avenue. Once all three friends were in, they turned to look at the stadium rising up around them. It was their first time looking up from the field instead of down from the stands.

"Wow!" Finn gasped. "The seats just keep goin' up and up 'til they hit the sky."

"I remember this one day in math class," James said, "we talked about this thing called infinity. It's when somethin' just keeps goin' and goin' forever. That's what all these seats feels like."

After staring at everything above, the friends looked down at the thick, green, outfield grass and reached down to touch it.

"There's more grass in this one spot than our whole neighborhood put together," Finn said.

James picked a few blades, put them in his pocket, and said, "If anybody asks if we really walked on Ebbets Field, I got proof."

Bobby looked over to the infield.

"Look how far that is," he said.

"Sure is a long way," Finn said.

"Let's see how long," Bobby said and took off running with Finn and James following.

Bobby ran all the way from right field to home plate, jumped on it with two feet, then turned and started running down the line to first base. Finn and James did the same. Bobby knew he should stay quiet so they wouldn't get caught, but as he rounded first and headed to second, he couldn't help himself. He lifted his arms above his head and yelled, "Home run for Bobby Kelly, and the crowd goes wild."

He could hear Finn and James laughing behind him and couldn't help laughing himself. Bobby kept going past second, around third and slid into home. He jumped up and yelled, "Dodgers win! Dodgers win!"

Finn came in, slid and jumped up and James slid in and just sat laughing on home plate. They were all tired from running and sat down to catch their breath.

Bobby closed his eyes and listened to how quiet the stadium was without a crowd.

He stood up and said, "It's so quiet in here, it feels like we's in church. Let's go play the infield. Who you wanna be?"

Whenever he played stickball, if Bobby got first choice, he always picked to have his team be the

Dodgers so he could pretend to be one of his favorite Brooklyn players.

"I call Pee Wee Reese at shortstop!" James called out.

"I'll play second and be Eddie Stanky," Finn said.

"I usually pick to be Dixie Walker in the outfield," Bobby said, "but today I'll play first base so we can turn some double plays. I ain't heard yet who's on first for Brooklyn this season."

"I ain't so sure Eddie Stanky and Pee Wee Reese is gonna be at second and short this year," Finn said. "I been readin' about this Negro the Dodgers signed. His name's Robinson or somethin' like that. He played second base in Triple-A Montreal last year and shortstop when he was in the Negro Leagues."

"Stop flappin' your lips!" Bobby yelled. "You tryin' to tell me some colored boy's as good as Pee Wee or Eddie?"

"Fuggetaboutit," James said. "No way is the Dodgers gonna let some Negro be in the startin' lineup. My dad says the coloreds ain't good enough to play with Major Leaguers."

"Ease up," Finn said. "I'm just sayin' what's in the papers."

Bobby didn't read the newspapers during the winter. There were no baseball box scores to go over with Dad, so he didn't bother.

"How can there be a Negro on the Dodgers when there ain't never been any coloreds in the Major Leagues?" Bobby asked. "A lotta people's gonna blow a fuse if this Robinson takes away a startin' job from a fella who already earned it fair and square."

"C'mon guys," James said. "We's playin' the infield at Ebbets Field. We got no time to waste yakkin' about stuff that probably ain't gonna happen anyways."

They all ran out to their positions. Bobby started calling out in his best Red Barber radio announcer voice.

"The Dodgers are up by one in the top of the ninth. The Giants are threatening with one out and a runner on first, but Brooklyn can win the game with a double play. Here's the pitch! It's a sharp grounder up the middle. Can Reese get to it?"

James ran over behind second and dove like he was going for a ground ball.

"Reese nabs it! He turns and gets it to Stanky covering second!"

Finn ran to where second base would be, and James made a throwing motion to him. Finn acted like he was catching it.

"Stanky turns and makes the relay throw to first base. Do they have time to turn two?"

Finn turned and pretended to throw to Bobby, who ran over and put his left foot where he thought first base should be. Even though Bobby was in the play now, he still kept being the announcer.

"It's gonna be a close one, folks! Oh no! The throw is a little up the line towards right field! The first baseman has to dive to catch it while still keeping one foot on the bag!"

Bobby dove into the dirt to catch Finn's pretend throw while still keeping his left foot down.

"He got it! That's three outs and the end of the game! Dodgers win!"

Bobby had real Ebbets Field dirt all over his clothes. It was a badge of honor. He rolled over onto his back and looked up at the blue sky while trying to think of a way to make it so Ma could never wash these clothes.

Then he heard a booming voice. A real voice. An adult voice.

"Nice play, kid!"

CHAPTER 2

"What-chu kids doin' here?" the voice boomed.

Bobby sat up and looked over at the first base dugout. The shouting was coming from a short, stocky, gray-haired, old man. One look at his grumpy face told Bobby he was just about ready to blow a fuse.

"Answer me! Why you kids in here messin' up the field?"

Bobby froze. He didn't know what to do.

"All three-a-youse get over here now!"

When Bobby got in trouble in the neighborhood, the first thing that always came to mind was ditching out and hoping he didn't get caught. If he took off now, he could get back out through the right field fence and run home before this old man could find him.

He looked back at the man standing on the top step of the dugout. It wasn't just any old dugout. It was the Dodgers' dugout. Bobby thought it he went over there, he'd at least get to see inside the dugout of his favorite team. He could always run away after he saw the dugout.

Bobby walked over and Finn and James followed. When he got to the old man, Bobby said, "Sorry sir. We didn't mean to do nuttin' wrong."

"The only time somebody says, 'I didn't mean to do nuttin' wrong,' is when they been doin' somethin' wrong!" the old man snarled. "You think we just let a bunch-a goof-offs come in here and mess up our infield whenever they want?"

Bobby stayed quiet and looked at his shoes. He knew he wasn't supposed to answer.

"Follow me," the old man said.

He turned and walked down through the dugout and into the tunnel behind it.

Bobby thought about running away again, but what was in that tunnel? It was where the Brooklyn players went after the game was over. He shot a look at Finn and James and nodded his head toward the dugout. He walked down into the dugout, and they fell in behind. Bobby started up the tunnel and saw the old man walking ahead and not looking back.

Bobby hoped they would go in the door with "Clubhouse" written on it, but the man walked past it to the end of the tunnel, up some stairs, and down a hallway. He finally stopped at a door with the words, "Brooklyn Baseball Club," and below in smaller letters, "Branch Rickey, President."

Bobby's Dad had told him about Branch Rickey hundreds of times. He couldn't believe he was standing at the door of the person Dad always called "the wisest man in baseball."

Any time Bobby and Dad talked about the Dodgers, Dad would say, "Brooklyn's got good teams even though we ain't got a lotta money like the Yankees. Them millionaires can buy their pennants, but Branch Rickey's gotta outsmart everybody to get ours."

The old man said, "Wait here," knocked on the door, and went in.

Bobby looked at Finn and James. He wanted to tell them he was sorry, but before he could say anything the old man came back out and said, "Mr. Rickey would like a word."

He pointed to the room and Bobby knew they were supposed to go in. He was excited and scared all at once. He was about to meet the great Branch Rickey, but the president of the Brooklyn Dodgers — the man who picked who got to be on the team — was probably going to tell him he was banned from Ebbets Field for life.

Bobby walked into the room, and there was Mr. Rickey sitting behind his desk. He'd seen Mr. Rickey's picture in the newspapers, but it didn't prepare him for what he saw now. Mr. Rickey looked huge, with giant, bushy eyebrows rising up above his glasses. He was wearing a suit and tie and had a cigar in his mouth. Bobby was already scared, and Mr. Rickey hadn't even said a word.

Those eyebrows shot up and his voice boomed out, "You boys — why did you break into my baseball field?"

"I'm really sorry, sir," Bobby said. "The whole thing was all my fault."

Bobby pointed at Finn and James and said, "They was just followin' me, sir. Please let 'em go. I'll take whatever punishment you got for all three of us."

Mr. Rickey look surprised.

"That's an admirable sentiment," he said.

Bobby didn't know what "admirable" or "sentiment" meant, but they must mean something pretty good because Mr. Rickey turned to the old man and said, "Show these two out."

The old man walked out to the hallway and motioned for Finn and James. The two boys stood frozen looking at Bobby. He nodded his head towards the door to let them know it was OK to go. They went out, and the old man shut the door.

Bobby turned back to Mr. Rickey, who asked, "What's your name, son?"

"Bobby Kelly, sir."

"Where do you live?"

"Flatbush, sir."

Mr. Rickey nodded and said, "Well, explain yourself, son."

Words started tumbling out of Bobby's mouth. Words were coming faster than his brain could think, but somehow he was still saying them.

"I'm really sorry. I know what I did was wrong, but I wasn't meanin' to do nuttin' wrong. I only done it because I'm the biggest Dodger fan in the whole world! I ain't seen Ebbets Field since last September, and it's my favorite place I ever been. My dad took me to my first Dodger game here when I was six years old back in 1941. Ever since that day, I always wanted to be part of the Dodger team in some way. I shouldn't have snuck in, but, well..."

Bobby stopped and took a big gulp of air to catch his breath. He couldn't think of anything else to say. He looked down at the ground and tried to get himself ready to hear Mr. Rickey tell him he could never come back to Ebbets Field for the rest of his life.

"I'm always glad to hear young people are fans of our team," Mr. Rickey said. "We can always use more fans."

Bobby looked up.

"If you want to be here so badly that you are willing to break in, maybe we should come up with a way for you to be here every day."

Bobby was confused. Adults never said things straight out. What did "be here every day" mean? Was Mr. Rickey giving him some sort of after-school detention? If coming to Ebbets Field every day was the punishment, Bobby didn't mind.

"The man who just brought you in here is our equipment manager. His name is Skip. He was just telling me earlier today that the bat boy from last year's team will not be able to come back for this season. Therefore, we will need a new bat boy. That sounds like just the job for the world's biggest Dodger fan."

Now Bobby was really confused.

"Do you...I mean...uhhh...sir, do you mean me?"

"Of course I mean you!" Mr. Rickey's voice boomed. "Did you not just claim to be the world's biggest Dodger fan?"

"Yes, sir."

"This way you'll get to be out on the baseball field every day — without having to break into the stadium first," Mr. Rickey said and let out a loud laugh. "The players get back from spring training next week, and we will have practice here on Monday afternoon. What time do you get done with school?"

"2:45, sir."

"Can you be here by 3 p.m.?"

Bobby thought for a second. To get to Ebbets Field by 3 p.m. on a school day he had to leave right when the last bell rang and run most of the way to the ballpark since he didn't have money to take the trolley. He had to leave before doing homework or chores, so Ma would ground him for sure, and then he couldn't be bat boy.

"Yes, sir. Yes I can be here by 3 p.m."

There was no way he was going to say no. He had until next Monday. He'd get something figured out with school and Ma.

"Good," Mr. Rickey said. "Check in with Skip when you get here. Any questions?"

Bobby had a million questions running through his mind. Where did they keep the bats? Could he talk to the players? How would he know which bat belonged to which player? But out of all the questions in Bobby's head, only one ended up coming out of his mouth.

"Mr. Rickey, is it really true there's gonna be a Negro on the Dodgers this season?"

The eyebrows shot up again as Mr. Rickey said, "A talented and honorable gentleman named Jackie Robinson will be trying to help us win the 1947 National League Pennant — if that's what you mean."

He looked at Bobby, who now felt bad he'd asked.

"Plan to be here Monday at 3 p.m.," Mr. Rickey said.

"Yes, sir."

"I'm not sure how you got in here, but to get out, turn left out of this door and the hall will take you out to the front gate. It's been unlocked all day."

He started laughing as Bobby walked out.

CHAPTER 3

Bobby walked out of the stadium and found Finn and James waiting on the street. He told them the good news, and they all ran home as fast as they could so they wouldn't get chewed out for being late to supper.

When they got back to their street, they quickly split up to the different floors of their building. Bobby ran up the steps of the front stoop, up two flights of stairs and opened the door to his family's two-bedroom apartment just as Dad was washing up after working construction all day and Ma was calling out, "Supper's ready!"

Bobby sat down with Ma, Dad, his little sister Katie and their baby brother Mikey. As the family ate the cottage pie Ma made, all Bobby could think about was how to tell Ma and Dad about his new job. Before he could think too long, Ma asked, "Where might have you been off to today, Bobby?"

"Me and Finn and James went down to Ebbets Field, but we ran home real fast so we wouldn't be late for supper."

"What shenanigans were you up to at Ebbets Field with them lads?" Ma asked. "Even I know the Dodgers ain't playin' yet."

Bobby shrugged.

"I ain't seen it since last September."

Bobby knew he'd better not say anything about sneaking in through the right field fence or his meeting with Mr. Rickey. It wouldn't be fair to get Finn and James in any sort of trouble. Still, he knew there was no better time to break his news.

"Turns out, when I get down there, the equipment manager's moving some bats and balls and stuff into the stadium. I offered to help him out and he says, 'Sure kid.' We get to yakkin' and he tells me the Dodgers need a new bat boy this season."

He stopped and looked at his parents. They just stared back.

"So … I'm that lucky guy."

Bobby broke into a smile, but he could tell right away Ma already had reasons to be against the whole idea.

"Oh my boy! How you gonna go back and forth every day and be down there for hours at a time and still get your homework and washing done?" she asked. "Go on and tell 'em to find somebody else to carry around their silly sticks. Why can't they just carry the bats themselves? They're grown men for cryin' out loud! The men who do hurlin' back in Ireland don't need no boys to carry around their hurley sticks!"

Before Bobby could say anything, Dad jumped in.

"Hang on now," he said. "That's grand there, Bobby. Now Ma, it sounds like the boy's got quite a chance here. You know how many kids around Brooklyn would give their eye teeth to be bat boy for the Dodgers? This ain't the kinda thing that drops in your lap every day.

"I been tellin' you, Ma, learnin' baseball is part of what it means to have a boy be a real American. You grew up in the Emerald Isle before comin' over here, but I grew up here in Brooklyn, and you gotta believe me when I tell you baseball's about a lot more than some fellas throwin' a ball around."

"How many games do the Dodgers play?" Katie asked.

"The whole season's 154 games," Bobby answered as he made a cross face at Katie to let her know she should stay out of it.

Ma shook her head. She still wasn't convinced. Dad jumped in again.

"Only 77 of 'em is home games and lots of 'em is on weekends. Dollars to doughnuts, there's times when the Dodgers is on the road for a week or more at a time, and Bobby don't gotta go in at all."

"What time you gotta run off on game days?" Ma asked.

"Three in the afternoon."

She gasped. Before she could say anything, Bobby jumped in quickly and said, "I'll do my homework and chores when I get back in the evenin'. Ma, I promise. Besides, from what I heard, when I'm doin' stuff for the players, they give me tips sometimes. It might even be a couple of bucks a week."

He'd heard this but wasn't sure about it. He hoped it was true. If it wasn't, he'd figure it out later.

Bobby then looked at his parents and said, "You two is always tellin' me I'm moochin'. I could use that money to help us out. I'm 12 now, you know. More than once you been sayin' I need to start chippin' in around here. We ain't the Rock-a-fellas, you know."

Ma, Dad and even Katie had a good laugh at that. Ma kept the family dimes, and any time anybody asked for anything that cost any amount of money, no matter how small, she always said, "We ain't the Rock-a-fellas, you know."

After they were all done laughing, Ma said, "OK. We'll give it a try it for a few weeks and see, but I ain't promisin' nuttin' beyond that."

After dinner, Bobby walked into the living room where Dad was looking at the newspaper. When it was baseball season, he and Dad would go over the Dodgers box score in the newspaper together every day. Dad would explain what the different numbers meant and tell Bobby the story of how the game went. Even if Bobby listened to Red Barber call the game on the radio earlier in the afternoon, he would still hang on every word Dad said. Nobody in the world knew more about baseball than Dad. It was Dad who took Bobby to his first game in 1941 when he was six years old and taught him to yell, "Youse can't beat Da Bums!"

Dad folded the newspaper over and handed it to Bobby. The headline read, "Rickey announces promotion of Jackie Robinson."

"Looks like they's gonna have that Negro around, at least for a little while," Dad said. "You better watch out."

"Sure," Bobby said, but he didn't know what Dad meant.

"If they got a Negro on the team, the stands is gonna be full of coloreds. That's the whole reason Rickey's doin' this, to get all the coloreds to buy tickets. They already got enough trouble at the ballpark without all these Negroes showin' up. There's gonna be trolleys and busses and subways full of Negroes comin' in from Bedford-Stuyvesant for the games. There's a reason Ma and me is always tellin' you to stay away from Bed-Stuy."

Dad shook his head and said, "I ain't sure Mr. Rickey thought through all the trouble he's makin' by signin' that colored boy. You see any fights or crazy stuff goin' on in the stands, you make sure you get in the dugout where it's safe. Got that?"

"Yes, sir."

"Good. I think this Robinson fella's gonna bring trouble no matter where he goes. Best just to steer clear."

Bobby nodded and said, "Yes, sir."

"Now, don't worry too much about it," Dad said. "After a month of hittin' .150, he'll go right back to the Negro Leagues where he belongs. Coloreds can't make it in the Major Leagues. They ain't got the toughness when the pressure's on.

"He'll be gone soon enough and things can get back to the way they's always been. The way they's supposed to be."

CHAPTER 4

After Bobby got done talking with Dad, he went out to the street while it was still light enough to get a game of stickball going. Stickball was the closest Bobby and his friends could get to playing real baseball.

There was no place to play baseball in their Brooklyn neighborhood. No lawns. No empty lots. No open spaces. Just brownstones with apartments, the stoops in front of the buildings, the sidewalks and the street. Brick, cement, asphalt and no grass.

Besides, nobody else on this street was a "Rock-a-fella" either. There was no money for extras like a baseball glove or bat, so the boys would get an old broom and saw off the handle to make a stick to hit with, then scrape together 10 cents and go to the corner store to buy a pink rubber ball called a "Spaldeen."

They would take the stick and ball and go to the one place they could find open space — the middle of the street.

Home plate was a manhole cover. First base was the garbage can in front of the market. Second base was a pot hole near the middle of the street. Third base was the Johnny pump, or fire hydrant. All they needed to get a game going was to get a few kids together.

The pitcher would throw the Spaldeen on one bounce to the hitter who would swing at it with the stick. Getting outs on fly balls and force outs was just like in baseball, but some things were different. A ball hit clear to the next manhole cover on the fly was a home run. If it was hit onto the roof of a building, it was a "hindoo" or do-over, and everybody had to wait until somebody went and found the ball. When the Spaldeen broke a window, everybody bolted.

The same day Bobby found out he was going to be bat boy continued to be perfect when he was able to get on the same team with Finn and James for stickball, and they picked to be the Dodgers. The other team picked to be the Giants.

The game was tied 3-3 as the sun was setting. They never kept track of innings. What stopped the game was if boys started getting called in for supper or if it got too dark to see the ball.

Bobby's team was just coming up to bat when Finn said, "Score's tied and we ain't never gonna get up to bat again before it gets dark. We gotta get some hits, and quick."

Bobby was up first. He reached in his pocket to grab the Claddagh ring and rubbed the heart for good luck. He didn't use it every time he went up to hit. Ma told him there was only so much luck in it and to only use it when he really needed it. A tie game in the last inning was one of those times.

He grabbed the stick and got into his batter's stance next to the manhole cover. The pitcher for the Giants, a kid named Johnny, turned to the other boys on his team and yelled, "Score's tied! Giants 3, Dodgers 3. Don't worry. I'm gonna strike all three of these dimwits out, and the game's gonna end in a tie."

It was the kind of thing Bobby expected Johnny to say. He was always busting somebody's chops. Even though they lived on the same street and were in the same grade at the same school, Bobby had never liked Johnny.

Bobby also didn't trust Johnny because he was a Giants fan. A Giants fan in Brooklyn! More than once, Bobby had yelled at Johnny, "Why don't you go cross the river and live in the Bronx and root for the Giants over there!" The only thing that would have been worse was if Johnny cheered for the Yankees.

Right now, Bobby wanted to yell back at Johnny, "If you don't stop flappin' your gums, I'm gonna give you a knuckle sandwich!"

He knew that wouldn't shut Johnny up, though. Getting mad and yelling was what Johnny wanted so he could throw Bobby off his game. The way to shut Johnny up was to get a good hit.

Johnny wound up and bounced the Spaldeen to Bobby. It was fast, but Bobby was ready. It came right down the middle and Bobby leaned in and gave it a good whack. The ball flew past Johnny and the fielder behind him and kept going up the right side of the street.

Bobby took off for the garbage can in front of the market that was first base. A couple of old men sitting on crates in front of the market looked up, started laughing and yelled, "Go, Kelly, go!" as Bobby flew by and turned for second.

The Spaldeen hit the curb on the right side of the street and bounced back to the middle of the street, so the player chasing it still couldn't get to it. Bobby touched second base that was a pot hole near the middle of the street and headed for the fire hydrant that was third base.

Katie and her friends playing hop scotch on the sidewalk all looked up as Bobby touched third. Now everyone out on the street was watching and shouting.

As Bobby rounded third he saw the fielder pick up the ball. He kept going as hard as he could to make it back to the manhole cover that was home. Johnny was standing in front of it, waiting for the throw. Bobby knew it was going to be a close play.

Bobby ran until he was two steps from home and jumped in the air trying to get to the manhole cover in one hop. As Bobby jumped up, the throw to Johnny came in low and he had to bend down to get it. As Johnny was down getting the low throw, Bobby sailed barely over the top of him and landed on the manhole cover before Johnny could bring the ball up and turn to tag him. Bobby hit the manhole cover with both feet then turned around and gave the "safe" signal with his arms.

"He's safe!" Finn yelled. "Dodgers win!"

Bobby, Finn and James started jumping up and down together, but Johnny was a sore loser. He had to put a kibosh on the whole celebration.

"You just got a lucky bounce," he said. "You didn't hit it all that far. That wouldn't have even gone past first base on a real baseball diamond like Ebbets Field."

"You don't know from nuttin'," Bobby shot back. "You ain't never even been down on the infield at Ebbets Field."

"So what?" Johnny said. "You ain't neither."

"Oh yeah? Me and Finn and James was down there today. We snuck in and ran all over the field."

Johnny shook his head and said, "I don't believe you."

James pulled the blades of grass out of his pocket and said, "Look. These is from there."

Johnny laughed and said, "Those could be from anywhere with grass! It's not like they got 'Ebbets Field' written on 'em. Bobby's lyin' and you're just followin' him."

"Don't call me a liar," Bobby said. He shoved Johnny and said, "Take it back!"

"Don't shove me," Johnny said and shoved Bobby back.

Both boys balled up their fists and glared at each other as a group of kids circled around waiting to see if there would be a fight. Bobby didn't want to end such a great day with a fight, but he couldn't back down. Anyone who chickened out from a fight on the street would be known as a coward.

Finn stepped in the middle and said to Johnny, "We can prove it. While we were there, Bobby got hired as bat boy for the Dodgers."

All the kids gasped and started whispering.

"Now you're just lyin' even worse to cover up the first lie," Johnny said.

"You wanna bet?" Bobby asked. "I'll bet you 50 cents, the price of a grandstand ticket, that if you come to a Dodger game you'll see me on the field as bat boy."

Bobby dropped his fists and held out his right hand so they could shake on it. Johnny put down his fists and shook Bobby's hand to make it a real bet.

As soon as their hands pulled apart, Johnny said, "Even if I do come to a game and even if you is the bat boy, I'm still gonna be havin' the last laugh because youse is gonna be pickin' up after that new Negro."

The kids stopped talking and looked at Johnny.

"Who's that colored boy they got comin' in to play this year?" Johnny asked.

"Jackie Robinson," Finn said.

"Yeah, him," Johnny kept going. "He's gonna drop his bat after he hits and look over at you and say, 'Fetch me my bat, white boy!'"

Johnny started laughing and looked around to see if he could get any other kids laughing.

"And you're gonna look up at him and say, 'Yes, sir. Right away, sir. Anything you say, sir!'"

He laughed even louder, and Bobby could hear other kids joining in.

"That ain't the way the world's supposed to work, Chief. If you're workin' for a Negro, maybe you need that 50 cents a lot worse than me."

Then he let out his biggest laugh of all and walked off up the street with a group of kids following him.

Bobby, Finn and James walked the other way and sat on the stoop in front of their building.

"Don't go listenin' to Johnny," James said. "He's a Giants fan for cryin' out loud. He don't know from nuttin'."

"Maybe he's onto somethin'," Bobby said. "It don't look too good for white people to go fetchin' stuff for coloreds. They's supposed to pick up after white people, like in the movies. Plus, my dad told me to stay away from Jackie Robinson, whoever he is."

"What did Mr. Rickey say?" Finn asked.

"I ain't so sure," Bobby said. "It sounds like he's pretty serious about havin' this Robinson fella on the team. What if he expects me to treat him like all the real players?"

"Good point," Finn said. "You don't wanna go gettin' fired right after you got the job."

"I got an idea," James said. "Why don't you just wait and see how the other players act around him? If they don't want him there, they's not gonna care what the bat boy does."

"That's pretty sharp," Finn said. "I was just readin' a newspaper article what says Dixie Walker and some of the other Dodgers wanna be traded rather than havin' to play with a Negro. The players know best. Wait and see what they do."

CHAPTER 5

On Monday, Bobby watched every minute tick by at school until the last bell rang. He shot out of the building like a rocket and ran every step as he made his way through Flatbush to Ebbets Field with his textbooks and homework under his arm.

When he checked in with Skip, the old man laughed and said, "You musta put on some kinda show for Mr. Rickey to go from bandit to bat boy in one day!"

That got Bobby laughing, too.

"I gotta bit a bandit in me too, kiddo," Skip said. "I think we's gonna get along great."

Skip showed Bobby around the equipment room and told him where everything went. There were stacks of bats, big piles of brand new baseballs, catcher's equipment and gloves. Bobby walked around amazed while taking in the smell of wood and leather. He never thought there could be so much baseball stuff in the whole world, never mind in one room.

"You gotta keep your eyes open around here," Skip said, "and make sure you keep track of everythin' in here. If you don't, stuff starts growin' legs and walkin' away, if you know what I mean."

They walked out of the equipment room which led into the clubhouse. The players were already out practicing, but Bobby could tell who had which locker because Skip had put a piece of tape with the player's name above each one. Bobby looked for "Reese," "Stanky," "Walker" and his other favorites as they walked by.

From the clubhouse, they walked down a tunnel to the dugout. As they came out of the dark tunnel into the sunlight, they both stopped to look around the stadium.

Skip shook his head and said, "I been doin' this job 30 years, but every day when I come out here I still gotta stop and look around this old place. Ain't no other spot like it on God's green earth, that's for sure.

No matter how many times I walk outta that tunnel, I ain't never gonna get tired of seein' Ebbets Field."

"I already feel like that and I'm only 12," Bobby said, and they both laughed.

Today, Bobby didn't have to imagine Pee Wee Reese and Eddie Stanky throwing the ball around because the real players were playing catch just 100 feet away.

Even though it was practice, the players had their uniforms on for team picture day. The white jerseys were so bright in the sun, Bobby had to squint to look right at them and read "Dodgers" written across the front. The hats were blue with a white "B" on them.

Bobby looked around to find all his favorite players but his eyes stopped on one player.

That Negro was here.

His dark skin looked different against the bright, white jersey. He looked like he didn't belong. All kinds of thoughts came rushing into Bobby's head. Johnny would make fun of him for picking up his bat. Dad told him to stay away from him. Mr. Rickey might be mad if he didn't help him. It only took a few seconds for Bobby to go from excited to confused. Why did this

Robinson fella have to come along and ruin everything for him?

Bobby didn't have time to worry about it because Skip broke his train of thought by saying, "Wake up, boy! It's time to get to work!"

He showed Bobby where everything was kept in the dugout. At one end was a rack of cubby holes where every player kept four or five bats with his uniform number marked on the bottom of each bat. When a player came in to take batting practice, Bobby would run over and find the player's box, grab two bats and take them to the player. He also had to keep track of the players' gloves and go pick up bats by the batting cage when players were done with them.

Things got so busy, Bobby didn't have time to get nervous about being around his heroes. Before he knew it, he looked up and saw Pee Wee Reese jogging to the dugout.

Bobby hurried over to the cubby holding bats with a "1" marked on the end, grabbed two and got back to the top of the dugout steps just as Pee Wee was arriving.

There he was. Right next to Bobby. Not down here while Bobby was 500 feet away up in the stands. Bobby didn't know what to do so he just held up the two bats. Pee Wee grabbed the bats, handed his glove to Bobby, smiled and walked off to the batting cage. It all happened so fast Bobby didn't have time to worry about any of it.

As soon as he put Pee Wee's glove away, Bobby turned to see Dixie Walker waiting at the top of the dugout steps.

"Hello there, young man," he said. He had a slow southern drawl just like Red Barber on the radio. "Could y'all grab me a couple of them bats?"

Bobby hustled over to the cubby holding bats with "11" on the end and ran back to the dugout steps.

Dixie grabbed the bats and said, "Thanks a bunch, son," and handed Bobby his glove.

"You're welcome, sir," was all Bobby da.ed say back.

"Y'all are new here this season?" Dixie asked.

"Yes, sir."

"What's your name, son?"

"Bobby Kelly, sir."

"Well Bobby-boy, welcome to the Dodgers."

As Dixie walked away to the batting cage, Bobby could hardly contain his pride. He was a part of the Dodgers! A real live Dodger just said so! He couldn't wait to tell Dad when he got home.

He went down into the dugout to put Dixie's glove away. Suddenly, out of the corner of his eye, he could see that face again — that face that didn't look right in a white Dodgers jersey with a blue cap. Bobby wasn't sure what to do. This Negro was new here, too. Maybe he wouldn't figure out it was Bobby's job to grab his bats. Maybe if Bobby just kept his back turned Robinson would think Bobby was busy and go get his own bats.

"Excuse me," Bobby heard him say. He turned around. This Robinson fella he'd been hearing so much about was standing there with a very serious look on his face.

"I'd like my bats."

He said it in a way that wasn't mean, but let Bobby know he was on the team and wasn't going away without his bats.

Bobby turned around and walked slowly to the bat rack. What was Robinson's number anyway? How was Bobby supposed to know if Robinson had never played for the Dodgers before? As he looked up and down the boxes, he heard Robinson say, "Bat 42."

Bobby found the box and grabbed two bats. He turned and walked slowly back to the dugout steps and held the bats out without looking up. Robinson grabbed the bats and slapped his glove in Bobby's hand in one motion. He was gone before Bobby could even look up.

After practice, Bobby had a lot to do around the clubhouse but couldn't help looking around to see where his favorite players had their lockers. He was carrying bats back through the clubhouse when he noticed that just outside the equipment room, the Dodgers had given the Negro a nail in the wall to hang his clothes on instead of a locker.

Bobby started arranging bats in the equipment room, but he could see out the doorway that Eddie Stanky was walking over to Robinson.

Eddie stared at Robinson, but he stared right back. Finally, Eddie said, "Before I play with you, I want you to know how I feel about it. I don't like it and I don't like you, but we'll play together and get along because you're my teammate."

Robinson didn't even flinch. "All right," he said. "That's the way I'd rather have it. Right out in the open."

They both looked at each other for a few more seconds before Eddie turned and walked away.

Bobby felt more confused than ever.

CHAPTER 6

The next day, Tuesday, April 15, 1947, was Opening Day for the Dodgers. Bobby could barely pay attention in school, and when the last bell finally rang he sprinted all the way down to Ebbets Field.

When he got there, there were more colored people than he'd ever seen at one time in his entire life. Many were dressed up nice like they were going to church or something. He'd seen Negroes at games before, but never this many. There were always Irish, Italians, Poles, Germans, Jews and all kinds of people at Brooklyn games, but never so many colored people as today.

When Bobby got inside Skip said, "There's one very important piece of equipment I been waitin' to show youse."

They walked into the equipment room, and Bobby saw a small Dodger uniform on a hanger.

"Oh my golly! Is that for me?" he asked.

"Course it is, kiddo," Skip said. "You can't be no real bat boy without one."

"It looks just like a real uniform!"

"That's cuz it is. Washed it special just today. I put extra bleach in it so it shines out in the sun.

"I'll step out and close the door so you can try it on."

He was halfway out the door before he stopped and turned back.

"Oh yeah. I almost forgot the best part. The outfit ain't complete without it."

He reached into a box by the door, pulled out a blue cap with a white "B" on it, tossed it to Bobby and walked out.

Bobby hurried and put on the uniform he'd been waiting his whole life to wear. Was this the "Heaven on Earth" Father O'Keefe was talking about during Mass last week? The uniform was heavy flannel he'd have to wear out in the hot sun, but he didn't care. There was no way he was taking it off.

Once he had the uniform and cap on, Bobby started taking bats out to the dugout. When he got out to the field, the stands were only about half full, and it looked like half the crowd was colored people. He could hear some of the players talking behind him as he put the bats in the boxes.

One of them said, "Rickey signs Robinson so he can fill the stands with Negroes, but when the stands get filled with Negroes white people don't want to come out. It's Opening Day, and the stadium's only half full. Doesn't seem like the smartest business plan."

The ballpark announcer came on over the public address speakers to announce the starting lineup.

"Batting first and playing second base, number 12, Eddie Stanky. Batting second and playing first base, number 42, Jackie Robinson."

Bobby nearly dropped the bats in his hands. Robinson was not only going to play, he was going to start and bat second in the order? Maybe they were planning to let him bat once to make all the Negroes happy then take him out.

"At least he's not playing shortstop," one of the Dodgers standing behind Bobby said to Pee Wee Reese. Bobby turned to hear what the Dodgers shortstop would say.

Pee Wee looked at the other players and said, "When I was coming home from World War II on a troop ship a couple of years ago, somebody came and told me the Dodgers had just signed a Negro. Then they told me he was a shortstop. My worst fear was I was going to have to go home to Louisville and have people tell me I wasn't man enough to protect my job from a colored boy."

Bobby looked around, and several players were nodding as Pee Wee kept talking.

"Then I started thinking, what if they said to me, 'Reese, you got to go over and play in the colored guys' league.' How would I feel? Scared. The only white guy. Lonely. But I'm a good shortstop, and that's what I'd want them to see. Not my color. Just that I can play the game. And that's how I've got to look at Robinson."

Pee Wee paused and looked around at the group of players.

"I know one thing," he said. "The smartest pitcher I ever faced was a Negro — Satchel Paige. I hit against him in an exhibition game. Make no mistake. These colored boys can play ball.

"You know, just one time in my career, I'd like to beat those Yankees. Maybe this guy can help us do that."

Pee Wee looked around at the group again, grabbed his glove and walked down to the other end of the dugout.

As Brooklyn took the field and Robinson ran out to first base, some of the Boston Braves players in the third base dugout started yelling at him. They were things Bobby had heard before from people around the neighborhood. Things and names people would say about Negroes, but not while a colored person was standing right there.

Robinson didn't say or do anything. He just stood there with the same determined look on his face as yesterday when he told Bobby to get his bats.

Skip came and stood behind Bobby in the dugout and listened.

"Boy, that's some pretty tough stuff," Skip said.

"You think he's just gonna stand there and take it?" Bobby asked. "In my neighborhood, if some wise guy's givin' you the business and you don't let him know you ain't afraid to give him a knuckle sandwich, he's gonna keep right on goin' 'til everybody on the street knows youse is yellow. Then you really got problems. I wonder why he ain't doin' nuttin'."

"He and Mr. Rickey made a deal," Skip said. "Robinson can't say nuttin' back to nobody. He can't get in no fights." He stopped and shook his head. "It sure ain't gonna be easy."

"What?" Bobby said. "Don't Mr. Rickey want somebody who's got the guts to fight back?"

Skip shook his head. "Mr. Rickey says he wants somebody who's got the guts not to fight back."

Bobby didn't have time to make sense of it because the Dodgers got three outs and were jogging back to the dugout. It was time for him to get to work. His first job was to make sure each player had two bats ready in the on-deck circle so he could warm up while he was waiting to hit. Bobby hurried and got two bats out for Eddie Stanky, the lead-off hitter.

Robinson was up next, and Bobby still wasn't sure what to do. He knew Dad wasn't at the game. Johnny probably wasn't at the game, or he would have made some wise-crack about it at school. Most of the players didn't seem to talk to Robinson or like him so they probably wouldn't care much if he told the Negro to go get his own bats.

But Mr. Rickey must be here. Was he sitting somewhere he could see into the dugout? He was the one who could fire Bobby if he wasn't doing the job the way he wanted.

When Boston pitcher Johnny Sain finished warming up, Stanky took one bat and headed to the batter's box and left the other for Bobby to pick up. As Bobby grabbed the bat from the on-deck circle, Robinson came up out of the dugout and looked at Bobby. It was the same look as yesterday. With anybody else, Bobby would have already had two bats out there in the on-deck circle, but he didn't have Robinson's bats ready.

Bobby reluctantly went down into the dugout and grabbed two bats with "42" on the bottom. He ran them up to the top-step of the dugout and handed them to Robinson, then hurried back into the dugout with his head down, hoping nobody saw him.

Stanky got out so Bobby ran out past Robinson to get that bat, then ran back into the dugout to get things ready for the No. 3 hitter.

As Robinson stepped into the batter's box, Bobby caught himself thinking, "I hope he gets out." He'd never thought that about any Dodger before.

Robinson hit the ball high in the air, dropped his bat by home plate and ran down to first base. It was a fly ball the center fielder was able to catch.

The wood bat with "42" on the bottom was lying there on Ebbets Field, and Bobby still hadn't figured out what he should do.

"Hey, Bobby boy!" Skip's voice boomed behind him. "That bat ain't gonna pick itself up! The bat boy picks up bats! Hurry up! Youse is holdin' the game up!"

Bobby hustled out of the dugout to pick up the bat with "42" on the end.

CHAPTER 7

The Dodgers beat the Braves 5-3. After the game, Bobby put everything away as fast as he could, changed out of his uniform, said so long to Skip then ran home lickity-split. He wanted Ma to see he wouldn't be too late getting home after games.

Ma kept a plate of boxty from supper warm for him, and Bobby did his homework at the table while he gobbled down his food. By the time he got done and got out to the street it was turning dark, and the stickball game was just breaking up.

When Johnny saw Bobby he tossed the stick at his feet and said, "Pick up my stick, white boy."

"The Dodgers won today," Bobby shot back. "I was hopin' to see you in the crowd so I could win our bet."

"I dunno how bad I wanna go watch those Dodgers," Johnny said. "They can't be that good if they's gonna let some Negro play for 'em."

He laughed and started walking away with some other kids following him.

"Just show up, then pay up," Bobby yelled after him.

Finn and James came over, and they all sat on the front stoop of their building while Bobby told them about his first game as bat boy.

"It was great, but I got one big problem," he said. "When that Negro comes up to bat, I can't decide if I want him to strike out or get a hit."

"If you're rootin' for the Dodgers, why would you want him to strike out?" Finn asked.

"Well, I want him to do bad enough they send him back to the Negro Leagues, and then he ain't gonna be around the Dodgers no more. That way I don't gotta listen to Johnny or worry about what Dad's thinkin'."

"Wait, you still want the Dodgers to win, right?" James asked.

"Course I do! That's the problem. Ain't never been no Dodger I didn't wanna cheer for before. I dunno what to do."

"I think you just gotta cheer for the Dodgers no matter what," Finn said. "How does Robinson act around the other players?"

"It's kinda weird," Bobby said. "Robinson's got this way of lettin' people know he ain't too happy with what they's doin' even though he don't say a word. He's got this stare he gives people like the glare the nuns give you at school when you ain't doin' your work."

James laughed and tried to do the look they'd all seen at school.

"Like today," Bobby said, "a bunch of the Braves was yellin' stuff at him, but he didn't do nuttin'. Just stood there and gave 'em a glare."

"Why don't he do somethin' about it?" James asked.

"Somebody told me Mr. Rickey made him promise not to get in no fights."

"That don't make no sense," James said.

Bobby just shrugged and said, "That's what I heard."

"Then why don't the other Dodgers do somethin'?" Finn asked.

"It ain't their problem," Bobby said. "They never asked to have him around."

Finn shook his head and said, "If Pee Wee Reese gets in a fight with somebody on the other team, the other Dodgers is gonna jump in and help him out just like you jumped in and helped me when I got in a scrape with that eighth-grader a couple of months back."

"I did that because we's buddies," Bobby said. "None of the Dodgers is buddies with Robinson."

"Yeah, but they's teammates," Finn said.

The next day at school Bobby's class went to Mass where Father O'Keefe taught them about the Gospels. Bobby liked the priest, who was also the headmaster, because he was a Dodger fan, too.

Last August on a Sunday afternoon, Father O'Keefe got up during the service and said, "It's too hot for a long sermon. Go home and pray for the Dodgers."

Bobby did just that. Maybe he needed to do it again to figure out this whole thing with Robinson. As Bobby was thinking, he heard the Father quote a scripture about "the sins of the fathers being visited upon the sons."

Bobby sat up and listened closer.

Father O'Keefe kept going and talked about a "scapegoat" that people put their sins on to have them taken away.

Finn raised his hand and asked, "Is that like if a fella plays a trick on a teacher, but then another guy gets blamed for it, and that guy don't wanna be no squealer so he shuts up and takes the punishment to help the other fella out?"

Bobby and Father O'Keefe both looked at Finn. Three months ago, Bobby put a spider in the top drawer of his teacher's desk. She blamed Finn because he was the last one up at her desk before she opened the drawer and started screaming. Finn knew Bobby put the spider there, but he also knew the code of the neighborhood was you didn't squeal on a buddy. No way, no how. He walked down to Father O'Keefe's office and took the punishment without saying a thing.

Bobby looked over at Father O'Keefe. Was he thinking about the same thing? Bobby raised his hand to ask a question and change the subject.

"Yes, Bobby," the priest said. "Do you have a question?"

"I can see why a fella's gonna take the blame to help a pal, but why's somebody gonna help people if they ain't even buddies?"

"Well, my boy," the priest said, "that's a good question. It's easy to see why most people would think that way. However, throughout history, there have always been people, very important people it turns out, who were willing to go through difficult times even though they didn't do anything to bring it upon themselves. They did this because they thought that, after it was all done, what they did might make the world a better place."

He stopped and smiled. Bobby still wasn't sure if he understood.

CHAPTER 8

After two more home games against the Braves, the Dodgers left Brooklyn and went up to the Bronx to play a weekend series with the New York Giants. Since Bobby hadn't played stickball all week, he couldn't wait to get back out on the street with Finn and James.

On Saturday the boys got a good game going. They played all morning and on through lunch. Only one thing could get Bobby off the street today.

That happened just before 1 p.m. when Bobby heard Dad call his name. He looked up and saw Dad leaning out the window of their apartment. He had a pitcher of lemonade in one hand and a radio in the other.

"Come up to Tar Beach!" he yelled.

Bobby yelled, "Gotta go," and sprinted off to his building before any of the other boys could get mad.

"Tar Beach" was what Dad called the roof of their building. It was covered in tar paper, but it was like a beach because people went up there on summer days to get out of their hot apartments and feel the cool breeze.

Bobby's favorite thing in the world was going with Dad to Dodger games at Ebbets Field, but his second favorite was when he and Dad would go up to Tar Beach with a pitcher of lemonade and listen to Dodger games on the radio.

Today they sat in the sunshine and sipped lemonade as they listened to Red Barber's voice coming through the speaker. They almost didn't even need the radio because when a Dodger game was going, people up and down the street had the radio on and their windows open, and anyone walking by could hear the game. Red Barber announced that the Polo Grounds, where the Giants played, had a record crowd of 52,000 people at the game.

"That's a lot of people," Bobby said. "That's more folks than they could ever fit into Ebbets Field, even if they packed 'em in like sardines."

Dad just nodded.

"It's probably mostly colored folks because of Robinson," Bobby kept going.

Dad just nodded again. He was usually the one who did most of the talking, and Bobby wasn't sure why he was being quiet today.

They kept listening, and when one of the Giants hit a ground ball, Bobby heard Red Barber say, "Reese throws to Robinson at first for the out." The way he said it, someone who was listening and didn't know the Dodgers team wouldn't even know Robinson was a Negro.

Dad said, "I don't think that colored boy ever played first base in the Negro Leagues or the minors. He always played second or short. He know his way around first?"

"I guess so," Bobby said. "He ain't made no stupid errors or nuttin' like that. Not yet anyways."

He stopped. He was all nervous inside. He wasn't sure what Dad was looking for. When Dad didn't say anything, Bobby kept going.

"I mean, he ain't great or nuttin', right?"

He waited to see what Dad would say. When he didn't say anything, Bobby added, "But he ain't really so bad at playin' first base."

They kept listening. The next inning Robinson came up to bat and got a hit.

"Why do they got him hittin' clear up at second in the order?" Dad asked, shaking his head. "He look like he knows what he's doin' when he gets up to bat?"

Bobby wasn't sure why Dad was asking him. Whenever they went to a game, it was always Dad who was telling Bobby who had a good stance, or waited for the right pitch or took a good swing.

When Bobby paused, Dad said, "I seen the stickball games you got goin' when I'm walkin' up the street on the way home from work. I seen you hit. I can tell you know how to swing. You seen this Robinson guy play, so I'm asking ya, can he hit or what?"

Bobby thought for a few seconds. He'd been hoping Robinson wouldn't be able to hit so he'd get sent back to the Negro Leagues. Now Dad was asking, and when he really stopped and thought about it, with a nervous tone in his voice he said, "Well, he looks like he knows what he's doin'. I mean, he's already got some hits, and he socked a homer in last night's game."

Dad said nothing and took another sip of lemonade.

Bobby kept listening and sipping his lemonade, but something didn't feel right. It wasn't the same as last season. He wished things with Dad were more comfortable, and they could go back to the way they were before Robinson came along.

CHAPTER 9

The next Tuesday the Dodgers opened a home series at Ebbets Field against the Philadelphia Phillies. When Bobby got to the stadium that afternoon, he saw Robinson had a real locker now instead of just a nail, but not much else was different. He still sat alone and nobody talked to him. Bobby got all the equipment out to the dugout just like before, but once things got going, it was a bit different than last week.

As soon as the game started, the Phillies, led by their manager, Ben Chapman, started yelling nonsense at Robinson, but it was more people yelling than last week, and some of the things they were shouting were much worse than before.

"They're waiting for you back in the jungle, black boy!" "We don't want you here!" "Go back to those

Negro Leagues where your type belongs!" Things about how he looked, his family and how he wasn't good enough to play with whites.

And there was one word they kept saying a lot. Bobby had heard people around the neighborhood say the word before when they talked about colored people, but he'd never heard somebody yell it right at a Negro.

Robinson was still just standing there doing nothing, just like last week. He had that same look on his face.

Bobby didn't like having Robinson around, but he didn't like what the Phillies were doing, either. It didn't seem like a fair fight. It was like a bunch of kids picking on just one kid. There were fights on Bobby's street all the time, but nobody liked a bully or a fight that wasn't fair. The Phillies were picking a fight with somebody who promised Mr. Rickey not to fight back.

In the bottom of the eighth inning, the Philadelphia pitcher threw one at Robinson and hit him in the shoulder, giving him a free pass to first base.

Bobby sat next to Skip and watched as the Phillies started yelling at Robinson as he trotted down to first.

"Those Phillies is actin' like a bunch of bullies," Bobby said. "I don't care what Robinson promised Mr.

Rickey, I wish there was some way he could get back at 'em."

"Just you watch, kiddo," Skip said. "He's about to drive every knucklehead on that team nuts."

When the pitcher went into his stretch and got ready to throw, Robinson started dancing off the bag. Bobby had seen players take a lead off first before. This was different. Robinson's feet were always moving. He'd go as far as he possibly could before the pitcher would turn and throw to first. Robinson kept going out farther and farther, but each time the pitcher threw over, he barely got back to the base in time.

"It's like he's measured everything down to the inch in his head," Bobby said to Skip. "I don't get why he's doin' all that fugazi stuff with his feet movin' all the time."

"Cuz the pitcher's about to burst a blood vessel, that's why," Skip said with a chuckle. "The pitcher's so worried about Robinson he ain't even thinkin' about how he's gonna get the hitter out. Robinson's in his head. I heard about him doin' this kinda thing in the Negro Leagues, but I didn't know he could put on a show like this here at Ebbets Field."

After throwing over to first a few times, the pitcher finally pitched the ball to the batter at the plate. Even though the pitcher, catcher and everyone in the Phillies dugout who was screaming at Robinson knew he was going to try to steal second, Robinson still took off for second.

He had such a good jump and the catcher was trying so hard to throw him out that the throw sailed way over the second baseman's head and into centerfield. Robinson slid into second, and when he saw the throw go into the outfield, he popped right up and got to third before the Phillies could get the ball back in.

"Wow!" Bobby said to Skip. "He never even hit the ball, but it's like he socked himself a triple."

Robinson then got enough of a lead off third he was able to score on a groundout, and the Dodgers ended up winning, 1-0.

When the game was over, Bobby hauled the bats, balls and equipment back into the equipment room. As he took things through the clubhouse it all seemed just like it was before the game. Robinson was still sitting by himself in front of his locker, and nobody was talking to him. Skip and Bobby could see him from the equipment room.

"Ain't never seen nuttin' like that," Skip said. "Usually, when a fella practically wins the game all by hisself, everybody comes by and slaps him and the back and says, 'Good game!'"

Bobby shrugged. "That's because none of these guys asked to have him here. He's only here because Mr. Rickey wants him here."

"The reason Mr. Rickey's got him here," Skip said, "is to help us win ball games, and he just went and won us a ballgame."

Bobby huffed and said, "If that's what he's here to do, then I guess he did his job today. It don't mean everybody's gotta go fallin' all over themselves to tell him how great he is."

Skip shook his head and said, "That ain't the point, kiddo. That's what they'd do for anybody else on the team. In case you ain't noticed — he's on the team."

Bobby wanted to yell, "Don't remind me!" but he didn't want to be rude to Skip. Instead he said, "I'm goin' out to the dugout and make sure I didn't leave no bats."

The next day started the same. Bobby got to the clubhouse and saw Robinson sitting by himself in front of his locker. When the game started, the Phillies yelled the same kinds of things as yesterday.

"That ball ain't no watermelon, boy!" "You can't play with white people! You know that!"

And they kept saying that one word over and over and making Bobby more and more uncomfortable. He'd heard that word more in the past two days than in the rest of his whole life put together.

In the bottom of the first inning, Eddie Stanky led off for the Dodgers and grounded out. Bobby ran out to home plate to pick up the bat with Robinson walking behind him to bat next. As Bobby grabbed Eddie's bat, he could hear the yelling start up again from the Phillies dugout. He was getting sick and tired of them. He didn't want to see Robinson give up the game because of garbage like this.

Bobby grabbed the bat and started walking back to the dugout. As he walked back he looked at Robinson coming the other way to get in the batter's box. Bobby could see something was different. Robinson didn't have his usual stare that showed everybody he was unhappy but keeping his emotions in check. This time he just looked angry. Was he mad enough he'd break his promise to Mr. Rickey?

Bobby hustled back to the dugout. Just as he got there, Eddie came up to the top step of the dugout. He looked over at the Phillies and yelled, "Hey you yellow-bellied cowards! Why don't you pick on somebody who can fight back!"

Everything went quiet.

CHAPTER 10

The Dodgers beat the Phillies 5-2 that day with Eddie Stanky getting two hits, Jackie Robinson scoring two runs and both being involved in two double plays.

When Bobby got home, Ma pulled a warm bowl of mutton stew and chunk of soda bread out of the oven and set it on the table.

"I told you, Ma, they got some food in the clubhouse I can eat after the game," Bobby said.

"Oh Bobby," Ma said, "I don't know if that food is what's good for ya. I know what I cook with here. Now go on, eat this. So, did your Dodgers win today?"

"Yes, Ma."

"The women around here don't usually say much about baseball, but a bunch of 'em has been talking about that colored boy playin' for Brooklyn."

Bobby knew how Dad felt about Robinson, but he'd never asked Ma.

"What-chu think about it?" he asked her.

"It wouldn't be for me to know," she said. "I don't much deal with this kind of thing, but it sure seems to me if they want him to be on the team they should be decent to him for cryin' out loud. Is the team treatin' him decent?"

"Kinda. Today the other team was yellin' some pretty rough stuff at him."

"Oh no. That's too bad," she said. "Think of the poor fella's family."

"He's got a family?" Bobby asked.

"Everybody's got a family, you silly lad. I ain't heard if he's got a wife or kids or anythin', but even if he don't, he's still somebody's son, ain't he? His poor ma probably gets sad when people yell such mean things at her son. I know I'd sure be sad if I heard people yellin' at you."

When Bobby got to the ballpark the next day, Skip was sitting in the equipment room sorting letters.

"Take a seat, kiddo," he said. "I already took the equipment out. Mr. Rickey wants us to sort out all these letters to Robinson."

"Sure is a bunch of 'em," Bobby said.

"I got 'em divided into three piles," Skip said. "The first pile is from people that like Robinson. The second pile is from people who don't think a colored fella should be playin' for the Dodgers. The third pile we gotta turn over to the cops."

"The coppers?" Bobby asked. "What for?"

Skip picked up the third pile and said, "These is from knuckleheads sayin' they's gonna kill Robinson if he keeps playin'. It's one thing if you don't wanna see a Negro playin' for the Dodgers, but youse gotta be some kinda nut job to to wanna kill somebody over playin' baseball."

He sighed and told Bobby, "Dig in."

Bobby opened envelopes and started sorting the letters into three piles. He found one that told Robinson to keep trying. The second one said Robinson should go back to the Negro Leagues. The third one was from someone who said they had a gun and they would shoot Robinson and his family if he kept playing. It was unsigned. Bobby felt scared just holding it.

He remembered what Ma said and asked Skip, "Robinson got a family?"

"Sure does. His wife Rachel comes to all the games to cheer him on and brings their baby boy with her a lot. Next time we's in the dugout I'll point her out. I gotta say, I feel bad for that lady having to sit there and listen to them idiots yellin' such garbage at her husband."

Bobby handed Skip the letter. Skip read it and said, "I can't even imagine tryin' to play ball in the Major Leagues while worryin' about somebody wantin' to shoot you. I dunno how Robinson does it."

After sorting the mail, Bobby went out to the dugout. He looked over and saw Robinson holding a baby and talking to a woman. It must be the family Skip was talking about. Robinson handed the baby to the lady and jogged over to play catch. He ended up standing right next to Pee Wee Reese.

Pee Wee laughed and said, "Get away from me you human target. Some crazy will take a shot at you and miss and hit me. I don't look good with holes in me."

For the first time all season, Bobby saw, not only was Robinson laughing, he was laughing with a teammate.

CHAPTER 11

The next time the Dodgers went on a long road trip, things went back to how they'd always been before for Bobby. He walked home from school, grabbed a chunk of soda bread Ma left on the counter for a snack, tended to his chores and homework then headed down to the street to see if anybody wanted to get a game of stickball going.

One afternoon Bobby was able to get his favorite set-up where he was on the same team with Finn and James, and they of course picked to be the Dodgers. Johnny was on the other team and, as usual, they picked to be the Giants.

When it was Bobby's turn to hit, he got in the batter's box and waited for Johnny's pitch.

Johnny got a smirk on his face and said, "So if this team's the Dodgers, I guess Bobby is that Negro what plays first base."

He turned around and laughed to his teammates and they laughed, too.

"What's it your business?" Finn yelled at Johnny. "Jackie Robinson's better than anybody on the Giants. So what if he's a Negro. He plays for Brooklyn, don't he?"

Bobby listened to Finn and wished he could think of something clever like that to say when Johnny started acting like a wise guy. All that was going through Bobby's head was wanting to sock Johnny right in the chops to shut him up.

Bobby stepped out of the batter's box for a few seconds and tried to shake it off. Then the idea of how to get back at Johnny came to him. If Johnny thought Bobby was Robinson, he'd show him what it was like to play against Robinson.

Bobby fixed his face with the toughest stare he could, then turned around and glared right at Johnny. He could tell by the look on Johnny's face he wasn't sure what was going on. Still he wound up and pitched, and when the ball bounced up to the plate, Bobby was ready for it. He knocked a clean single between second and third.

When Bobby got to first base that was the garbage can in front of the store, he started dancing away from the can, moving his feet in the pigeon-toed way Robinson did. Johnny looked over his shoulder to see what was going on. There was no stealing in stickball because there was no real catcher, but Bobby could still tell Johnny wasn't sure what to do.

Finn was up to bat. Johnny kept looking at Finn, then back over at Bobby, then back at Finn. He couldn't decide who to worry about. He finally threw an easy pitch that Finn slugged down the third base line.

Bobby rounded the pothole in the middle of the street that was second base and looked to see that one of the Giants had picked up the ball and another was covering the fire hydrant that was third base. It would be a close play either way, but if he was going to be Robinson, he was going to make the other team make a good play to get him out. Bobby took off for third, and when he got a couple of steps away, he saw the ball go bouncing past the Giant covering third. The other team was so worried about catching him, they made a bad play.

Bobby jogged home easily and turned and glared at Johnny.

CHAPTER 12

Jackie Robinson hit well for the first few games of the season but then went into a slump. Fly outs. Pop outs. Ground outs. Strike outs. He just kept getting out. He'd come back to the bench and sit by himself. Bobby would look at him and wonder if he'd get sent back to the Negro Leagues. At the beginning of the season, he hoped Robinson would get sent away, but now he wasn't sure how he felt.

It didn't help that the whole Dodger team was in a slump or that every time Bobby saw Johnny on the street or in the school yard Johnny would yell things like, "How's your Dodgers doin' now with that colored boy on first base?"

The worst times were when Johnny would yell things in the school yard in the morning while they were waiting for the first bell to ring. There was nowhere to go to get away from it. At first, Bobby tried to ignore it and hoped Johnny would get bored and stop, but every time Brooklyn lost another game and Robinson went 0-for-4 again, Johnny would say something, and every time it seemed like there were more kids joining in laughing after he said it. Pretty soon, Johnny had a whole group that would follow him around and laugh when he yelled things to Bobby.

Bobby couldn't think of a single wise-crack to say back. The Dodgers were losing, and Robinson wasn't hitting so what could he say? Besides, Johnny made him so mad he couldn't think straight.

It all kept building day by day. One morning Bobby walked into the school yard, and Johnny walked by and called out, "I saw your Dodger Negro went 0-for-4 again. Why can't your very favorite player get any hits, Bobby?"

Bobby turned and said, "Ya startin'? I'm gonna flatten youse!"

Bobby dropped his books, and as they hit the ground he socked Johnny right in the nose. Once his first punch connected, he didn't wait to see what

Johnny would do. He was so mad he just kept punching and punching. The only thing he could hear in his brain was, "Shut up! Shut up! Shut up!"

He felt Johnny hitting back sometimes, but he was so mad he didn't care. He just wanted to make him stop. Suddenly, Bobby couldn't feel Johnny hitting back any more and his punches were just hitting air.

Bobby looked down and saw Johnny on the ground with blood coming out of his nose. A group of kids was gathered around them, and Bobby looked up in time to see Father O'Keefe coming through the crowd.

"What in heaven's name is going on here?" the priest yelled.

Nobody said anything.

"Look at the state of you two," he said, shaking his head. "You hoodlums come with me. I'll sort you two lads out."

When they got to the headmaster's office, Father O'Keefe took Johnny in first while Bobby sat and waited on a chair outside the door.

After a few minutes, they came out and Father O'Keefe told Sister Mary Margaret to take Johnny to clean the blood off his face and shirt and put a patch on his nose. Father O'Keefe turned to look at Bobby, who got up and walked into the headmaster's office and sat down without having to be asked.

The priest sat down behind his desk and said, "What's wrong with you, lad? Did you give yourself a double-dose of original sin this morning? I've heard Johnny's side of the story. What do you have to say for yourself?"

Bobby stared at the floor. He wasn't sure what to say or do. While he was still looking down he heard Father O'Keefe say, "Don't mind being bothered by Johnny. A Brooklyn boy who says bad things about any of the Dodgers? It's like being Catholic and saying you don't like the Pope!"

Bobby looked up. The priest smiled and said, "Heaven knows, Johnny will have to answer for the sin of not cheering for the Dodgers when he meets St. Peter at the Pearly Gates, but it's not your duty to make him pay for it here on earth."

He stopped and looked at Bobby. Being in the office wasn't anything new to Bobby, and he knew what came next.

"I apologize, Father," Bobby said. "I'm ready to accept my punishment."

"Before we get to that," Father O'Keefe said, "is this everything this fight was about, or is there more to it?"

Bobby looked at the priest, again not sure what to say. Finally, he said, "Well, sir, I don't know if you heard, but I'm bat boy for the Dodgers now. Johnny's been teasin' me about havin' to pick up bats for that colored fella playin' first base."

"Oh, I see," Father O'Keefe said. "Does it bother you that he makes fun of you, or that he makes fun of the Dodgers for having Jackie Robinson play first base?"

Bobby shrugged and said, "I dunno. Guess I never tried thinkin' about it like that."

"No matter what it is Johnny says to make you angry, what did our Lord teach us to do when someone makes us angry?"

"Turn the other cheek," Bobby said, but he couldn't help adding, "but that don't always work out too good when you gotta deal with a kid like Johnny."

Father O'Keefe chuckled and said, "Let's look at it another way. What did doing a number on Johnny's nose accomplish today?"

"He shut up. That's for sure," Bobby said and sat up straight in his chair.

"Might have even shut that boy up for good," Father O'Keefe said with a smile.

Bobby smiled back. It seemed like the priest was starting to make sense. However, Father O'Keefe shook his head and said, "Even if you shut up Johnny for the rest of his days on earth, do you think you changed how he feels about a Negro named Jackie Robinson playing first base for the Dodgers?"

Bobby shook his head no.

"Our Lord taught us that love would win over our enemies better than hate. He didn't always teach us the easiest way, but he did teach us the best way."

Bobby nodded to show he understood, but he wasn't sure he did.

Father O'Keefe waited a few seconds, then said, "Now, despite this talk we've had and my understanding of the situation you were in, the penance for starting a fight in the school yard is staying one hour after school every day for one week."

"No!" Bobby gasped. "Anythin' but that! The Dodgers got a home stand all week. If I have to stay late every day I'll never get down to Ebbets Field on time, and I'll get fired as bat boy. Johnny got me so mad I forgot about gettin' in trouble for startin' a fight."

"Now, there, there, my lad," Father O'Keefe said. "My goal isn't to get you fired. We should be proud that of all the schools in Brooklyn we have the Dodgers' bat boy as one of our students.

"We don't want to ruin that, but as headmaster of this school I need to make sure you have a consequence for starting that fight. I could send a note home to your parents asking for suggestions, or I could call up the Dodgers, let them know what happened and ask them to come up with something."

Bobby didn't even need a full second to think about it. He almost shouted, "Please, make it the Dodgers. Not Ma and Dad."

"It's settled then," Father O'Keefe said. "You go get yourself looking suitable and head back to class, and I'll place a phone call to Ebbets Field. Who knows? Maybe

I'll even get to talk to Branch Rickey. I've got a couple of ideas about the pitching rotation."

He chuckled as Bobby left the office.

CHAPTER 13

When the last bell rang at school that afternoon, Bobby hurried out and ran down to Ebbets Field, not sure what would be waiting for him when he got there.

The moment Bobby walked in the door, Skip said, "Mr. Rickey would like a word, kiddo."

Bobby nervously walked up the stairs and down the hall to Mr. Rickey's office. The door was open, but he could hear Mr. Rickey talking to a group of newspaper reporters gathered in the office so he waited outside.

One of the reporters asked, "Branch, do you regret shaking up all of baseball to sign a Negro?"

Without missing a beat, Mr. Rickey said, "All I did was hire a superbly talented player to help the Brooklyn

Dodgers win a championship. It makes sense baseballogically."

The reporters laughed.

"Are you making up words again?" one asked.

"I think it's a very fine word," Mr. Rickey said.

"But Branch," another reporter said, "it doesn't seem like the other players are really accepting Robinson. Don't you think that's bad for team chemistry? We've been hearing that some of them might even refuse to play."

"Some players with us may quit," Mr. Rickey said, "but they'll be back in baseball after they work a year or two in the cotton mill."

Everybody laughed.

"Now gentlemen," Mr. Rickey said, "I don't want to keep you from the important work you need to do in the press box before the game."

As the reporters filed out of the office, Bobby heard one say to another, "What we should really be asking is, 'When is Robinson going to start hitting?'"

After everyone cleared out, Bobby went and stood in the doorway. Mr. Rickey looked up and said, "Come in."

Bobby walked over and stood in front of the desk and thought about how it was the second time in one day he'd been sent to the office for being in trouble.

"I received a phone call from Father O'Keefe at your school," Mr. Rickey said. "He tells me you were involved in some sort of school yard fisticuffs today."

"Yes, sir," Bobby said while staring straight ahead and trying to make the most serious face he could. "I got into a scuffle with a Giants fan who was sayin' bad things about the Dodgers."

Bobby could see Rickey's huge eyebrows rise up as he took the cigar out of his mouth.

"That's no excuse, son!" his loud voice boomed. "If I fought with everyone who says horrible things about this organization, I'd never stop fighting."

Bobby kept staring straight ahead, not sure what to say or do next.

Mr. Rickey continued, "The headmaster told me this may have had more to do with you being teased about being associated with our first baseman, Mr. Robinson."

Now Bobby looked right at Mr. Rickey. He couldn't believe Father O'Keefe told him about that, too.

"I want to make it very clear," Mr. Rickey said, "I will not have anyone in this organization, from the president," he pointed to himself, "down to the bat boy," he pointed at Bobby, "getting into fights about Jackie Robinson. It has never been part of our plan. I won't have anyone get into fights to defend Robinson, but I won't have them be ashamed of him, either. We are proud to claim such a fine man as a member of this organization."

Bobby nodded to show he heard what Mr. Rickey said.

Mr. Rickey leaned back in his chair and said, "Father O'Keefe also asked that I fashion some sort of appropriate punishment for you to discourage fighting in his school yard. I told him I would be happy to undertake such an assignment.

"In light of today's events, I think it would be a good idea for you to get to know Mr. Robinson so you can understand just how lucky we are to have him on our team.

"For the next two weeks, I want you to make him your number one priority. I want you to not only take care of his equipment the way you do for everyone else,

I also want you to stop by his locker every day and ask him if there is anything else he needs. I also want you to be on the lookout for things he needs and make sure you get them without him having to ask. I am giving you the job to do more than anyone in the entire organization to make Mr. Robinson feel like he's part of our Dodger team."

"Yes, sir," Bobby said.

"Oh, and one other thing. I do not want Mr. Robinson to know anything about this. Is that clear?"

"Yes, sir."

"Now, I won't keep you from the important work you have to do in the dugout before the game. So, skedaddle."

Bobby hustled from Mr. Rickey's office down to the equipment room and got everything out to the dugout. When he went back in the clubhouse he was nervous, but knew what he had to do. He slowly walked over to Robinson's locker, took a deep breath and said, "Do you want me to oil up your first baseman's mitt before the game?"

Robinson turned to him with a puzzled look on his face. Bobby's head was spinning, but he knew he had to keep going if he wanted to keep his job.

"Just want to make sure it's soft for the game, s…, ummm…yeah."

Bobby almost said "sir" to Robinson, but caught himself at the last second. It was a good thing Dad wasn't around. He'd make Bobby quit the bat boy job right then and there.

"Sure, that would be good," Robinson said and reached into his locker to grab the glove. As he handed it to Bobby he said, "You've got a cut on your lip. It looks like you got in a fight."

Bobby nodded and said, "Yeah, this stupid Giants fan at my school's been shootin' off his yap about the Dodgers so I had to pop him one, you know?"

As soon as it came out of Bobby's mouth, he knew how it sounded, and he wanted to take it back. Why did everything with Robinson, even just talking, have to be so hard?

He started to say, "Sorry. I know you promised Mr. Rickey no fighting," but he stopped when he saw Robinson chuckling.

"You know about that, too?" Robinson said with a smile.

Bobby nodded.

Robinson stopped smiling and his face got serious as he said, "Sometimes, for one wild and rage-crazed minute, I'll think, 'To hell with Mr. Rickey's noble experiment.' I am after all, a human being. What am I doing turning the other cheek as though I'm not a man? Some days I just want to stride over to the other dugout, grab one of those cowards yelling at me and mash his teeth with my despised black fist."

Bobby's jaw dropped. He couldn't believe what he was hearing.

"That's exactly how I felt in the school yard this morning," Bobby said. "I felt just like that when I went over and punched that kid right in the schnoz. How do you keep from throwin' punches at everybody?"

Robinson shook his head and said, "I just have to remember that this season isn't just about me and what I want right now. It's about a lot of people. It's about what I want this country to be like when my son grows up."

He stopped for a second before he got the smile back on his face and said, "But it sure would be nice just once to knock some sense into somebody the way you did today."

They both started laughing. Maybe this punishment wouldn't be so bad after all.

CHAPTER 14

When Bobby got home that evening, Dad was sitting on the couch with the newspaper reading the box score of the game Bobby had just been at.

"Dodgers lose again," Dad said. "Robinson hitless again. What's goin' on down there at Ebbets Field? Is it as awful as it looks in the box score?"

Bobby shrugged and said, "They's slumpin' right now. Seems like the whole team's havin' a rough go of it. No use givin' 'em the shoe leather and kickin' 'em when they's down. There's still plenty of games to catch up."

"Hope they start doin' it before Saturday," Dad said. "I got the day off and I'm comin' down to Ebbets Field to see my son be the one-and-only bat boy for the Brooklyn Dodgers."

He smiled at Bobby who did his very best to smile back even though in his head there was nothing but worry. What if Dad came to the game Saturday and saw Bobby being extra helpful to Robinson after Dad clearly told him to stay away from him? Maybe he could just not be so helpful just for that one day. But what if Mr. Rickey saw Bobby wasn't helping Robinson? The adults always made things so hard to figure out. Why did Robinson being on the Dodgers have to make everything so confusing?

Dad turned the newspaper to a new page and said, "Then again, maybe Robinson's a good luck charm. If the other team don't show up because they don't wanna be on the same field with a Negro, that means the Dodgers win by forfeit. Here, take a look at this."

He folded the paper over and handed it to Bobby. The headline on the story read, "Cardinals threaten strike." Bobby started reading about how some of the St. Louis Cardinals were threatening to strike rather than play against the Dodgers if Robinson took the field.

"Can they really do that?" Bobby asked.

"Read this paragraph down here," Dad said and pointed.

It was a quote from Ford Frick, the president of the National League, stating, "I do not care if half the league strikes. They will be suspended, and I don't care if it wrecks the National League for five years. This is the United State of America, and one citizen has as much right to play as another."

Bobby looked up at Dad and said, "So probably no strike. So Robinson's probably gonna be around a while."

He said it half hoping Dad would finally get used to the idea.

Dad just smiled and said, "I can see why the Cardinals don't wanna play on the same field as a Negro, but it's mighty chicken of 'em to just not show up. They should act like they was brought up better than that.

"Mr. Rickey already told 'em, if they don't show up it's a forfeit, and the rule book says the official score is

Dodgers 9, Cardinals 0. I hope those Cards show up anyway, and Brooklyn shows 'em where they gotta go and wins 19-0."

Bobby was able to smile at that.

CHAPTER 15

The next day, Robinson struck out his first time up and went to sit at the end of the bench. Bobby ran out to pick up Robinson's bat. As he jogged back to the dugout, he saw Mr. Rickey sitting just a couple of rows behind the backstop. It felt like he was staring right at Bobby. When Bobby got back in the dugout he went down to where Robinson was sitting and asked, "You want any water or anything?"

"Fastball low and outside," Robinson said as he looked past Bobby and out to the field at the other team's catcher. Bobby turned to look and the next pitch popped the catcher's mitt low and outside.

Bobby turned and looked at Robinson. He nodded to Bobby and said, "Next one's a curve ball."

The next pitch started high before breaking off and ending up down by the batter's knees.

"How you doin' that?" Bobby asked.

"I always study the other team's pitchers," Robinson said. "I try to figure out what they're going to throw in different situations. A lot of times you can see patterns they have with the catcher, or you can tell by the way they hold the ball or the angle of their arm when they release it."

He paused for a second, then said, "On this next one he's going to try to paint the inside corner."

Bobby watched, and Robinson was right again.

"Baseball's a game you have to study," Robinson said. "It's not just about running around and getting your uniform dirty. Now they're going back to fastball low and outside."

That was exactly where the pitch went, and the batter flied out. Bobby ran out and grabbed the bat as quickly as he could then hurried back to go sit by Robinson.

"If you don't mind me askin'," Bobby said, "If you know what pitch is comin', why ain't you hittin' it more?"

Robinson nodded and said, "Remember what I said before? Baseball's about using your brain, but you also have to get your body moving in the right way. I'm also thinking about using a different size of bat."

"We just got a new shipment of bats," Bobby said. "You want I should put some aside?"

"I've been thinking about going with one that's a little bit shorter but also a little bit heavier," Robinson said.

"After the game's over, I'm gonna grab just the bats you're talkin' about and write '42' on the bottom so nobody else can swipe 'em."

Right then the next hitter popped out to end the inning. Bobby didn't want their talk to end, but he knew he and Robinson both had to get back to work.

The next day was Saturday. Bobby planned ahead and tried to get as much done as he could for Robinson before the game since he knew Dad would be in the stands today. Bobby didn't want to be too close to Robinson out on the field or in the dugout unless he absolutely had to.

He brought Robinson the bats he marked with "42" the night before and said, "I bet you can get lots of hits with these."

Robinson smiled and said, "I think you're right. Now that the weather's warming up I can feel it. I'm going to start hitting. In fact, before I left today, my wife Rachel told me she could feel I was going to get a hit today."

"She come to the games?"

"Yes, and sometimes she brings our son."

Bobby remembered what Ma told him.

"She sure must get mad when she hears people yellin' at you and callin' you names."

Robinson chuckled and said, "My Ray is one strong woman. She can hold her own."

He picked up one of the bats with "42" on the bottom and said, "Do any of your family ever come to the games?"

"My Dad's comin' today. It's the first time this season he could get off work."

"Does your dad follow baseball?" Robinson asked.

"Sure does," Bobby said. "He taught me to be a Dodger fan. My Ma is from Ireland and she don't know nuttin' about baseball, but Dad's always tellin' her baseball's the best way to figure out what America's all about."

Robinson looked at Bobby and said, "I hope he's right — someday."

Bobby nodded, not sure what to say or do next. Finally he asked, "How's that bat feel?"

"Great," Robinson said, still working the bat in his hands. "Your dad must be proud of you. You're lucky to have your dad. I never got to know my dad. You make sure you mind him."

"Yes, sir," Bobby said. As soon as the "sir" came out of his mouth he hoped he wouldn't slip up any more today with Dad around.

Bobby turned to walk away, but Robinson said, "Hold on a minute."

Bobby turned back.

"Now that you got me these new bats," Robinson said, "I guess I won't be needing this old one I've been keeping in my locker to practice my swing with. Would you like it?"

Robinson held out the bat and Bobby took it.

"Wow!" Bobby said. "Nobody on my whole street's got any kinda bat at all. We just play stickball. Now I'm not only gonna be the only one with a real bat, it's a real bat that a real Dodger used!"

Robinson laughed and said, "Well, I hope you get more hits with that old bat than I did."

Bobby took the equipment out to the dugout and started looking around to see where Dad was sitting. He hoped he wouldn't be sitting where he could see into the dugout. Was Mr. Rickey at the game today? Was Johnny? Who should he worry about most?

The first time Robinson came up, the other pitcher threw at him and hit him. Robinson jogged down to first and then started doing his crazy feet dance off the bag. Bobby had been around Robinson on the bench enough to know he studied every pitcher and knew down to the inch just how far he could lead off first and still get back safe before the pitcher threw over to pick him off. It wasn't so far that he would get caught, but it was just far enough that if the pitcher wasn't careful, Robinson would take off and steal second.

On the third pitch, Robinson took off and swiped second easily. Then Dixie Walker hit a single and Robinson ran to third and home to score the first run of the game.

Two innings later, Robinson pulled one into the gap in left-center field for a double, stole third and scored on a sacrifice fly by Dixie.

Robinson got another hit in his last at-bat, and the Dodgers won easily. Bobby was happy they won and even happier nothing happened where Dad might see him helping Robinson.

CHAPTER 16

After that game, Robinson started tearing the cover off the ball, and the Dodgers started winning. Even better, Bobby wasn't having to listen to Johnny shoot his mouth off anymore. Maybe it was because the Dodgers were winning. Maybe it was because he went after Johnny. Bobby didn't care either way, as long as Johnny kept his pie-hole shut.

The Dodgers took off on a weeklong road trip, and Bobby was excited to play stickball again. He hurried home after school, did his homework and chores as fast as he could, then hustled downstairs to see who else was ready to play.

When he got out to the street, only Katie and some younger kids were sitting on the stoop. As Bobby walked down the steps, the kids near Katie got up and hurried away.

"Where they off to so fast?" Bobby asked Katie.

"They's scared," Katie said.

"Of what?"

"Everybody's scared of you since you beat up Johnny. They's goin' around sayin' you're a bully."

"Who's sayin' that?" Bobby said clenching his fists. "Tell me and I'll go clean their clock."

Katie laughed and said, "You're gonna go beat 'em up to prove you're not a bully?"

"I ain't no bully," Bobby said and sat down next to Katie. "I only slugged Johnny because he was askin' for it."

"That don't matter," Katie said. "If everybody on the street says you're a bully, you're a bully."

"How do I let everybody know I ain't no bully?"

"How should I know?" Katie said. "You're my big brother. You figure it out. Not for nuttin' do I gotta tell you, the problem ain't gonna get fixed by goin' around beatin' kids up."

Katie got up and walked down the steps to play jacks with a friend. Bobby just sat and thought about his problem because none of the kids his age were out yet.

A few minutes later he saw Johnny come out of his building. Johnny got to the bottom of the steps of his front stoop, pulled a Spaldeen out of his pocket and started playing stoop ball. Bobby played stoop ball when he was alone. You threw the ball so it bounced off the front of one step, down onto the top of another step, then popped back out to you. When Bobby got a good rhythm going it was hit-bounce-catch, over and over.

Johnny went for several minutes without missing before the ball finally bounced away and over by the stoop where Bobby was sitting. Bobby jumped up and went and grabbed the ball.

Bobby held the ball up and said, "When you gonna pay me that 50 cents you owe me for when we bet on me bein' bat boy for the Dodgers?"

Johnny shrugged and said, "I ain't never seen it with my own eyes. Far as I know, you're just makin' the whole thing up."

"I should just keep this Spaldeen as a 10-cent deposit on what you owe," Bobby said.

Johnny just glared and said, "What-chu gonna do if I say no? Try and beat me up again?"

"I won't have to try that hard," Bobby said. "Anyways, why you gotta be like that? The only reason I punched you was because you wouldn't shut up about Robinson. Not for nuttin' do I gotta say, Johnny, you can be a real pain in the neck."

Bobby bounced the ball to Johnny. He caught it with one hand and said, "Even if you beat me up 100 times, it won't change the fact the Dodgers got you goin' around pickin' stuff up for a Negro."

"So what if I am!" Bobby yelled. "Robinson's better than anybody you got on the Giants. What you shouldn't like about Robinson ain't that he's colored, but that he's gonna help the Dodgers beat the Giants and win the pennant. Besides, he ain't such a bad guy once you get to know him."

"Oh, so now you're hangin' out with Negroes," Johnny shot back. "Your dad know about that?"

"Oh shut up," Bobby said. "I dunno if you noticed, but ever since Robinson started playin' first base for the Dodgers, the world ain't stopped turnin'. My head ain't exploded. Baseball ain't got destroyed. It's all the way it was before except for one guy playin' for the Dodgers."

"You knucklehead," Johnny said. "It's all different now. My dad says now that they got a Negro on the Dodgers, the coloreds is gonna start wantin' to get in everywhere. They's gonna try and move in on our street and live in the same buildings with us."

"That's crazy talk," Bobby said.

"It don't sound too crazy to me. Whatever it is, you ain't helpin' the situation."

They both stopped and glared at each other. After a minute Bobby said, "How's about we make a deal? Leave me alone about Robinson but say whatever you want about the Dodgers. Just like last year."

Johnny thought about it for a few seconds before saying, "I guess so."

Bobby reached out his hand and they shook to make it a real deal.

"One more thing," Bobby said. "It ain't no fun beatin' you at stickball if you ain't yellin' about how your team is gonna beat my team the next game. At least yell that you're gonna strike me out or somethin'."

"I'll strike you out anyways," Johnny said. "So I might as well let everybody know about it."

CHAPTER 17

When the Dodgers got back to town, they had a series with the Cardinals. On Friday afternoon, Bobby got down to Ebbets Field and saw some kids had set up a table to sell Dodger buttons. Fans could buy and wear a button to let everyone know who their favorite player was. Bobby had always wanted one, but in past years he'd only ever had enough money to get a ticket into the park.

He walked up to the table and one of the kids said, "Got any favorites? We got 'em all here. Pee Wee Reese, Eddie Stanky, Dixie Walker, we even got a whole new bunch of Jackie Robinson buttons. They been sellin' like hot cakes."

Bobby looked down and saw a row of buttons that read, "I'm rooting for Jackie Robinson."

"You gonna buy one?" the kid asked.

"Maybe after the game," Bobby said and headed into the stadium.

As Bobby got the bats sorted out in the dugout before the game, he could see kids from all over Brooklyn looking over the edge of the dugout and reaching down with pens and balls, hoping that one of the Dodgers would grab them and sign an autograph.

Bobby was used to it by now, and if he had time would sometimes even help a kid get a ball to a favorite player for a signature.

Suddenly, he heard a kid yell, "Hey, there's Robinson!" A couple of seconds later he looked up and saw kids looking down yelling, "Jackie! Over here! Hey, Jackie!"

Robinson smiled and reached up to sign a few of them before an usher came and told the kids to leave so the Dodgers could get ready for the game.

St. Louis was the team that threatened not to play if Robinson was on the field. Then they found out the National League wouldn't support them, and Mr.

Rickey would claim the game as a forfeit win for the Dodgers. The Cardinals showed up to play, and the minute Robinson got on the field the St. Louis team let him know they weren't happy about him being there. It kept going throughout the game.

About mid-way through, Bobby sat down next to Skip on the bench and said, "It ain't as bad as what the Phillies was yellin', but it still don't feel right."

"I heard it's been like this on the road," Skip said. "They shoulda figured out by now they ain't gonna drive him away that easy."

"I just wish somebody else on the team would do like what Eddie Stanky did with the Phillies and go yell at 'em and tell 'em to knock it off," Bobby said.

Just then the Brooklyn pitcher gave up his third hit in a row, and the manager walked out to remove him and bring in a reliever. While the players were waiting for the reliever to come in from the bullpen, Robinson was standing there, and the yelling started up again. Bobby looked up and down the bench to see if anybody was going to do anything, but nobody was moving.

He looked up and saw Robinson standing there with his usual stare, but then he saw somebody moving. Pee

Wee Reese was walking over to where Robinson was. He put his arm around Robinson's shoulder and started talking to him.

The Cardinals dugout went silent.

The Dodgers won, and as Bobby was taking the equipment through the clubhouse after the game he heard Dixie Walker tell a reporter, "Nobody's done more for the Dodgers this year to help us get into first place than Jackie Robinson."

As he walked by Robinson's locker, he noticed players were coming by to congratulate him and slap him on the back.

Bobby finished up as quickly as he could and hurried out of the clubhouse exit the players used when they left Ebbets Field. It was faster than going out the front, and Bobby liked seeing the fans waiting to congratulate the players after a win.

There were usually little groups gathered around different players, but today there was a group so big Bobby could barely get by them. He wasn't tall enough to see which player was attracting all those fans, but as he got a little farther away he could see into the middle of the group. It was Robinson. The black face that Bobby thought looked so out of place on the first day of practice now looked just right in a sea of faces of Irish, Italian, Polish, Jewish and Negro fans all gathered around and reaching out to Robinson.

CHAPTER 18

On Saturday morning, Bobby got up and had breakfast just as Dad was leaving for work. Bobby spent the morning doing his chores and was just getting ready to leave for the ballpark when Dad came back in the front door and said, "The bad news is my shift got cancelled so no overtime pay. The good news is, now I can go to the game today."

Bobby tried his best to smile and said, "Gotta go," as he headed out the door.

"Meet you out front after the game," Dad called to Bobby as he left.

When Bobby got to the clubhouse he walked over to Robinson's locker and said, "Hey Mr. Robinson! You want I should sharpen up them cleats before the game?"

Robinson smiled and said, "Mr. Rickey finally told me about your punishment."

Bobby was so embarrassed his jaw dropped.

Robinson chuckled and said, "Mr. Rickey brought it up to me yesterday. He wanted to make sure you were doing what you were supposed to. He also told me the terms of your punishment ended last week, but it seems you're still doing extra things to help me out."

Bobby shrugged and said, "It's OK. I know I don't gotta do it. I'm only offerin' because I wanna help you so you can help the Dodgers win."

"All right then," he said, and handed Bobby his cleats. "But no more Mr. Robinson. Do you call my teammates Mr. Reese and Mr. Stanky or Pee Wee and Eddie?"

"Pee Wee and Eddie."

"Then just call me Jackie."

Bobby got the bats set up before the game and stood at the top of the dugout steps looking around at the whole field. He didn't look into the stands to see where anyone was sitting. He just looked at the field and marveled at the grass. It was just as green as the day he'd snuck in with his friends just before the season started. The thought of it put a huge smile on his face.

Skip came out and saw him and said, "Somebody looks happy."

"The field looks great," Bobby said. "I know 'Da Bums' is gonna win today."

"That's the spirit," Skip said. "It's nice to see you feelin' happy out here for once."

"Huh?"

"Sometimes when we come out here before the game I see you lookin' around in the stands and and lookin' a bit nervous. Why you gotta do that?"

"I worry sometimes about who might be watchin' me and what they might be thinkin'," Bobby said. "But you know what? I don't care no more. I don't care who's watchin' or what they's thinkin'."

Skip laughed and said, "Feels good, don't it?"

Bobby nodded and smiled.

Once the game got going, things went fine until the top of the third when the Dodgers were in the field.

One of the Cardinals hit a grounder to Pee Wee who grabbed it and threw over to Jackie at first base. The hitter was out, but when he got to the bag he put the metal spikes of his cleats down on the ankle of Jackie's foot that was on first base, even though he wasn't supposed to step on Jackie's side of the bag.

All season long players had tried to hurt Jackie, and all season long Jackie acted tough, like nothing happened. This time, Bobby could tell right away Jackie was hurt.

Jackie started hopping around, and the other Dodgers started running over to the St. Louis player who spiked Jackie. Players came out of both dugouts, and there was lots of pushing and Brooklyn players yelling at the Cardinals that they'd better leave Jackie alone.

Bobby stayed in the dugout, but off to the side he could see Jackie hobbling along, and he could already see a big red spot on his sock. Bobby grabbed a towel and went running out on the field. He could hear the Dodger fans booing the Cardinals and yelling at them.

He got to Jackie and looked down at the back of his ankle. The red blood stain was mixing in with the white of his socks and the blue of his Brooklyn stirrups. Bobby knelt down and pressed the towel against Jackie's ankle.

"You OK?" he asked.

"I'll make it," Jackie said. "Let me see if I can walk."

Bobby moved the towel and stood up as Jackie limped away. After a few steps of walking slowly he was able to walk faster, then run very slowly, then run normally. When he took a few running steps the crowd cheered, and the other Dodgers moved away from the Cardinals and came over to wish him well.

Jackie turned to Bobby and said, "Thanks," and Bobby ran back into the dugout.

The game stayed close until the bottom of the eighth inning, and Jackie was up to bat first.

Bobby wanted Jackie to get a hit because he was mad about what the Cardinals did. He wanted Jackie to get a hit because he wanted Dad to see that he could really play ball. He wanted Jackie to get a hit because now he was one of Bobby's favorite players on the team. Most of all, he wanted Jackie to get a hit because he wanted the Dodgers to win.

Bobby reached inside the back pocket of his bat boy uniform pants and pulled out his Grandpa's lucky Claddagh ring. He looked at the crown and heart being held between two hands. He rubbed the heart and squeezed the ring tight, closed his eyes and whispered, "Jackie, get a hit."

He opened his eyes, and on the first pitch, Jackie slapped a single into right-center field.

As the right fielder chased it down, Jackie took a big, wide turn past first base. He got halfway between first and second and skidded to a stop. He turned to go back to first, and the crowd groaned. He'd gone too far!

Now the right fielder had an easy throw to get him at first base. But as soon as the right fielder let go of the ball, Jackie turned and ran to second. He'd tricked the right fielder, and he was going to get to second easily!

The crowd realized it as soon as he took off and started cheering. It was the loudest Bobby had ever heard it at Ebbets Field. By the time the throw came in to first, Jackie was already to second.

Jackie got over to third on a ground ball, and when the next hitter came up, he started dancing off the bag, just like he did at first base.

In the dugout, Bobby turned to Skip and said, "With that tore up heel, he shouldn't be bouncin' around so much. Besides, what's he gonna do? Steal home? Nobody can steal home."

Skip just shrugged, but down the bench Bobby could hear the players saying things like, "If there's anybody who could do it, Jackie could." "I heard he stole home in the Negro Leagues."

Bobby watched the pitcher wind up. As soon as he let the ball go, Bobby saw something out of the corner of his eye. It was Jackie running down the third base line — and he wasn't stopping.

It turned into a race to see if Jackie could beat the ball to the plate. It was going to be close. About two steps from home, Jackie dropped down into a slide. The hitter moved out of the way and the catcher came up out of his crouch to catch the pitch. The ball was just high enough that Jackie got under the catcher and touched the plate a split second before the catcher got the ball and brought it down for the tag.

The umpire signaled safe, and Ebbets Field went wild. Bobby couldn't even hear himself think.

Jackie jogged back over to the dugout, and his teammates gathered round to congratulate him. Once he got settled back on the bench, Bobby walked over to him and said, "I didn't even know a fella could steal home. How'd you even know to do that?"

Jackie just smiled and said, "Above anything else, I hate to lose."

CHAPTER 19

After the game, Bobby took his time putting everything away. He was nervous about walking out of the stadium and meeting Dad. He had to have seen Bobby helping Robinson when he got spiked out on the field today. Bobby wasn't sorry about what he did, but he was worried the first thing Dad would say to him was that he couldn't be bat boy any more.

However, when Bobby finally got out to the street, Dad smiled and said, "That was some game, son! I never seen anybody play like that Robinson fella. I can't believe the way he baited the right fielder into throwing to first base, and then to steal home! I heard about Ty Cobb doin' it, but I ain't never actually seen it. I gotta admit, that Robinson fella's got brains for baseball and guts for the game."

They started walking home.

"After watchin' him play, I think I'm glad they's got Robinson on the Dodgers," Dad said. "I mean, I ain't sure about him comin' to my house for dinner or livin' on my street or nuttin' like that, but I'm sure glad he's on the Dodgers."

For the first time all season, Bobby took a deep breath of relief. He finally felt like things with Jackie and the Dodgers were going to be all right.

GLOSSARY OF SLANG

We thought that you 21st Century kids might not know some of the words and phrases in this book since they were used clear back in the 1940s. We wanted to make sure you know a "knucklehead" from a "knuckle sandwich," so we put together this glossary. That's a fancy way of saying, "Here's what some of this stuff means."

Blow a fuse - When somebody — especially an adult — gets really mad.

Burst a blood vessel - Same as "blow a fuse."

Bustin' chops - When you're busting somebody's chops, you're giving them a hard time.

Clean your clock - A threat to somebody who's bothering you that they'd better leave you alone, or else. "Watch out or I'll clean your clock!"

Da Bums - What Brooklyn fans called the Dodgers. Believe it or not, they meant it as a compliment. It was their way of saying that the Dodgers were Brooklyn's very own team.

Dimwit - What you call somebody when you think they're not acting too smart.

Dollars to donuts - When you want to say you're sure of something. "Dollars to donuts, the Dodgers will win tomorrow."

Don't go breakin' the Devil's dishes - Don't push your luck.

Eye teeth - Something very rare or valuable that you would give away to get something you really want.

Fella - Guy. Can be a man or boy. More than one is "fellas."

Flappin' your gums - Talking too much. "Stop flappin' your gums!"

Fugazi - Crazy or weird.

Fuggetaboutit! - Forget about it!

Givin' him the business - If somebody is bothering or teasing somebody else. "He's givin' him the business."

He don't know from nuttin' - He doesn't know anything.

Johnny pump - Fire hydrant.

Kibosh - Put an end to something.

Knuckle sandwich - Punching someone in the mouth.

Knucklehead - A name you call someone when you think they aren't acting very smart. "Hey you knuckleheads, stop goofin' off!"

Lickety-split - Really fast.

Moochin' - Getting something without paying for it.

No use givin' 'em the shoe leather - Don't kick someone when they're down.

Not for nuttin' do I gotta tell youse - I have to tell you.

Nuttin' - Nothing.

Pie-hole - Mouth.

Pop - To hit someone.

Rock-a-fellas - A reference to the "Rockefeller" family. They had lots of money.

Schnoz - Nose.

Shenanigans - Mischief or doing something silly. "What sort of shenanigans are you boys up to?"

Shut your yap! - Be quiet.

Skedaddle - Get out of here.

Stuff starts growin' legs and walkin' away - Things get stolen.

Tar Beach - The roof of a brownstone or apartment house.

Weasel deal - When a situation goes bad.

What's-a-matta? - What's the matter?

What-chu-doin'? - What are you doing?

Yakkin' - Talking.

Yellow - Afraid of a fight.

Yellow-bellied - Same as "yellow."

Youse - Another way of saying "you."

NOTES

While Jackie Robinson's historic rookie season with the Brooklyn Dodgers in 1947 actually happened, and many of the characters included in this book were real people, *Brooklyn Bat Boy* is a work of fiction. The character of Bobby Kelly is fictitious as are all of his interactions with the real people in the book, such as Jackie Robinson.

The terms "Negro" and "colored" are used in the book because they were terms that would have commonly been used in 1947. These terms are considered offensive today.

ABOUT THE AUTHOR

Geoff Griffin has worked as a lawyer, special education teacher, journalist and editor. He has over 20 years of experience writing for a variety of newspapers and magazines. He has published essays in a number of anthologies and is also the co-host of the award-winning Travel Brigade Radio Show and Podcast. This is his first work of fiction.

CPSIA information can be obtained
at www.ICGtesting.com
Printed in the USA
FSOW02n2022101116
27253FS

9 781530 482672